THE
JOAN
WALSH
ANGLUND

STORY·BOOK

Random House New York

Library of Congress Cataloging in Publication Data
Anglund, Joan Walsh. The Joan Walsh Anglund storybook.
SUMMARY: A collection of brief stories and poems on a variety of subjects.
[1. Short stories. 2. American poetry] I. Title. PZ7.A586Jo [E]
78-55913 ISBN 0-394-83803-3 ISBN 0-394-93803-8 lib. bdg.
Manufactured in the United States of America   1 2 3 4 5 6 7 8 9 0

A
TABLE OF
CONTENTS

These were stories I told at bedtime
to my granddaughter, Emily,
during her third summer on Nantucket
and so...
to EMILY
this book is lovingly dedicated in
grateful memory of all the happy island
hours we have spent together.

A TRUE TEDDY·BEAR

Once there was a little boy, and sometimes he was sick and had to stay in bed a lot. The only thing that would make him more comfortable was to have his big teddy bear tucked in beside him. That was just fine, but after a while the teddy bear began to get a little worn-out from all that snuggling. So finally the little boy's mother said she would have to mend it.

She sewed Bear neatly with strong yellow thread and soon he looked much better. But a little while later, one of his ears came off, so the mother said, "Don't worry, I will fix it."

She sewed on a new ear made of soft red cloth, and the teddy bear looked almost as good as new.

But then one day Bear's leg got ripped, so the mother took out her sewing basket and made a new one. But the new leg didn't quite match because it was blue.

Then, because the little boy sometimes used Bear as a pillow to prop up his head, the teddy bear's tummy began to sag, and the mother had to open him up in order to fill him with new stuffing.

While she was doing this, she had an idea.
Why not give Bear a heart! He already had
a lot of love inside, but it would be even nicer
if he *really* had a heart!

So the mother cut out a heart
shape from some cardboard,
and the little boy colored it all red
with crayons, marked down the date
on the back, and wrote the word
L O V E across the front. Then he
popped the heart inside the teddy bear's chest.

The mother put on a fresh brown-felt tummy and sewed it
up with pink thread. Bear was fit as a fiddle again.

Since then, several years have passed, and the little boy has grown taller. He doesn't get sick as much any more. So Bear doesn't need to sleep in the bed any more, and he doesn't get worn-out the way he used to. Now Bear sits safely on the shelf with all the Special Things that the boy wants to save. But Bear's smile is just as brave as it always was...and his little cardboard heart is just as full of love. And even though none of him quite matches any more, you can tell that once someone must have needed and loved him very much.

And that's what teddy bears
are *for*...after all!

FIVE LITTLE DUCKLINGS

Five little ducklings
      out for a swim.
One paddled off.
      (What became of *him*?)
The next got an ache
      and had to go home.
That left three
      to gambol and roam.
The third got frightened
      when the sun had set.
The fourth caught cold
      from the damp and the wet.
One little duckling,
      all too soon,
Swimming alone, by the light of the moon.

THE BIG BROWN BAG

It was a BAD DAY!
    Emily was hiding.
    She didn't feel like speaking,
        and she didn't feel
            like listening.

Under a big brown bag
    (with two holes poked through
        for looking and breathing)
          Emily was hiding.

Emily was angry at the world,
    and the world was not too pleased with Emily.

It was only ten o'clock in the morning,
    and already she had spilled her milk
    and broken her cup.

She had yelled at her brother...

. . . thrown her doll
across the room . . .

. . . and ripped her favorite book.

And *now* she felt unfriendly
and friendless.
So Emily was hiding.

The Brown Bag sat very still on the floor.
Not a sound.
Not a "sorry"
whispered out.

No! Emily was definitely HIDING!

But, slowly,
    a furry paw reached under
        the BIG BROWN BAG!

And then...
        a furry head peeked under,
        and a tiny pink tongue
            began to lick Emily's
            tear-stained cheek.

The Brown Bag quivered.
        The furry tail waggled.
        And, suddenly, there was EMILY!
The Brown Bag
        was tossed into the corner...
and the kitchen was filled
        with giggles...
            and meows...
                and hugs!
Emily was *back* again to stay.
It was a *happy* day after all!

STARS

The star looked down
    at the deep, dark sea
And he thought to himself,
    "Is that a twin to me,
Shining so brightly, there below?"

And he pondered,
    and then he decided, "No,
That couldn't be true,
    for I'm so high.
. . . And, besides, all *stars*
    live up in the sky!"

And the starfish, below,
    looked up to the sky.
"Why, that's a brother of mine,
    pinned up so high!"

But then he thought,
    "How could that be,
For everyone knows
    stars live in the sea!"
So both stars fell asleep,
    each in his blue,
And neither one questioned
    . . . so neither one knew!

GRANDMA SHIVERS

Once upon a time. . .
> there was a tiny little old lady
> who lived in a tiny little old house,
> and her name was Grandma Shivers.

> She was named Grandma Shivers
>> because she was always *cold*.

She was *so* cold
> she couldn't get out of bed
> in the morning!
So her house never got cleaned,
> and the rooms were thick with dust.

Her garden
> didn't get watered,
>> so all her plants
>>> drooped and died.

And she was so cold and shivery
> she became very cranky, and no one
> wanted to be with her.

She shooed away the birds
who came for crumbs.

She swept away the mice
who came for cheese.

And she *never* gave cookies
to the children
who came to call.

The little old lady
just sat, all alone,
in her little old house
and *shivered*
all by herself.

Then, *one* day—one rainy day—she heard a tiny sound at her doorstep. When she opened the door, in walked a tiny thin black kitten that was shivering *more* than Grandma Shivers.

That little kitten looked so wet and miserable and shivery that Grandma Shivers didn't have the heart to turn him out. So—in spite of herself—she bent down and gave that thin little black kitten a nice warm saucer of milk.

How that kitten purred!

Then Grandma Shivers lifted
    the little kitten
    up in her arms.
She cuddled it,
    and petted it,
    and sang it little songs,
    until it stopped shivering
    and fell fast asleep
    right in her lap.

So now Grandma Shivers
    doesn't shiver any more.
She just sits in her house,
    and rocks in her chair,
    and pets her little kitten,
        and *smiles*.
Because a little kitten,
    and a little love,
    can warm even
    the *coldest* heart!

21

JOHNNY·CAKE

Little Johnny Cake
    lived in a johnnycake house
    that his mother had baked.
Little Johnny Cake was very happy,
    but he did have *one* bothersome problem!
Mrs. Johnny Cake had baked such a *beautiful* house
    and such a *delicious* house
        out of johnnycakes
    that *everyone,* for miles around,
        came to nibble at little Johnny Cake's
        johnnycake house!
And so by sunset, each and every night,
                Little Johnny Cake didn't have
                a house at all . . . only a huge
                    pile of crumbs!

22

So every morning, bright and early,
　　Mrs. Johnny Cake would have to start all over
　　and make *another* house of johnnycake
　　　　for her little boy.

Then, one day,
　　Little Johnny Cake had a good idea!
He thought to himself, "Everyone likes johnnycakes
　　so much. Instead of baking just *one* johnnycake
　　house each day, let's bake *two* johnnycake houses!"

So now, every morning, Mrs. Johnny Cake bakes
　　two johnnycake houses—
　　one for her own little Johnny Cake to live in,
　　and *another* for all of his hungry friends to share.
Now, EVERYONE is satisfied, because—
　　"Yum, yum, yummy!
　　　　Johnnycakes are *good*
　　　　　　for your tummy!"

And, maybe, if you *ask* her, *your* mommy could bake *you*
　　a johnnycake too.

THE CURIOUS ADVENTURE OF LITTLE FISH

"Mommy, what is that green light up there?"
  asked Little Fish one morning
  as he was swimming to school.
"Nothing, my child. . . . Nothing,"
  answered his mother.

"But, Mommy, look!
  I see a shadow," said Little Fish.
"Hush, now, and swim, Little Fish. Swim right
  next to me," said his mother. "These waters can
  be dangerous, and we must stay together!"

But Little Fish was curious.
And when little fish are curious
  sometimes they forget
  to be wise.

So Little Fish, forgetting all about his mother's warning,
began to swim...but not next to his mother.
Instead he swam *up*—
up through the deep, dark, cool water...
up toward the pale green light...
up...up...up...
toward the tantalizing shadow.

He was almost there...when, *splash,*
he heard a bubble burst right next to him.
There, hanging from a string,
and wriggling in a most delightful way,
was the pinkest, wiggliest,
most delicious-looking worm
that ever a hungry little fish did see!

"Why, how nice!" thought Little Fish. "I'll just nibble
that little worm a bit for lunch. Mother won't
know...and it's such a *little* worm....
Surely it won't spoil my appetite!"

So Little Fish popped that wriggly pink worm right into
his mouth and started to swim back to his mother.

But, oh! All of a sudden, instead of
        going *down* as he had intended,
        Little Fish was being pulled up...
        up through the silver water...
        and out into the strange new world of air.
Plop! There he was in the bottom of a boat.

Little Fish was frantic!
        He couldn't breathe.
                The air was so strange
                        to his little fish gills.
        He couldn't see.
                The sun was so bright
                        on his little fish eyes.
        He was very frightened!
                He wanted his mother,
                        and he wanted
                        the nice, safe sea world
                        that he had always known.
                                Poor Little Fish!

Then, just above him, a loud voice said:
"Too bad...it's only a *little* fish!
...Much too small to keep.
Better throw him back!"

With a toss and a splash,
Little Fish went back where he belonged.

And ever after,
that's just where he stayed—
close to his mother,
swimming happily
in his own nice, cool,
green-water world.

...And he never went exploring again!

THE GREAT BIG GREEN WAVE

The tide rose up
    in one green foaming wave,

and it rolled up the beach,
    where it picked up a sea shell

. . . and a little tin shovel
    and a small painted pail

. . . and a floppy
    straw hat.

Then it spilled
    some driftwood
      on the sand.

Farther on, it spilled some green seaweed.

And then the great big green wave
grew even *bigger* and braver.
And it marched right up the sand
even faster and higher
till it touched a picnic basket.

And it tickled a gull
that was dining there

. . . and it rolled out a peach
that was lying by the basket.

. . . and it tipped over
a yellow umbrella

. . . and carried off a bandanna
someone had left behind.

And then . . .
 that BIG GREEN WAVE,
 so bold and so strong,
 strolled lazily down the sands again
 till it found the ocean.

Then it jumped right back in
 with a big white SPLASH,
 and disappeared forever.

So no one could ever find it,
 or blame it,
 for all the naughty things
 it had done!

A PUMPKIN STORY

PHONE CALL FROM A GRANDDAUGHTER, FAR AWAY

Hello, Nana. I *miss* you!
Hello, Grandpa. I *love* you!

I saw a cow in the field
today. He was eating grass,
and I gave him some clover
and he ate that too.

I drew a picture for you
in school. The teacher liked it.
I brought it home, and Mommy
is going to mail it to you.

32

I went to a birthday party. They gave me a balloon, and I got to wear my new, shiny shoes.

My cat had five kittens. . . . Do you want one?

When are you coming to visit me?

THE DEEP DEEP WHITE

They were playing
. . . in the Deep Deep White.

They were sleighing
. . . in the Deep Deep White.
They were rolling
. . . in the Deep Deep White.

They were throwing
. . . in the Deep Deep White.

They were hiding
. . . in the Deep Deep White.

They were sliding
. . . in the Deep Deep White.

They were building. They were running.
They were laughing. They were grinning.
        All in the Deep Deep White!

But then they shivered
. . . out in the Deep Deep White.
And they quivered
. . . out in the Deep Deep White.

So away they scurried
. . . away from the Deep Deep White.
And in they hurried
. . . in from the Deep Deep White
. . . next to the Warm Warm Fire.

And they sipped from the Hot Hot Chocolate!

A CHRISTMAS STAR

Once there was a little star.
Not a star up in the sky.
No, this little star was
        a *paper* star!
Once it had been all golden and
shining and had proudly perched
on top of the merriest Christmas
        tree in town.
But now the little star was
tarnished, and old, and quite
forgotten. . . . Now it was packed
away in the attic in a big box
with other forgotten things.

Poor little star!
     How dark it was in there!
         . . . And how dusty, and how lonely!

How it longed to see the snow again,
     to hear the tinkle of sleigh bells,
         to smell the scent of green pine boughs
          and crackly fires.

All through the long, dark months, it had dreamed
of all the Christmases it had known, Christmases
     full of laughter and songs, tinsel and candles,
     and happy, loving friends.

But now, in the deep shadows of the attic, the little star looked at itself. "Who would ever want me on their Christmas tree?" it thought sadly. "I'm so battered and tarnished. I'm not shiny at *all*! And my golden sparkle is gone. . . .What good is a star that can't *shine*?"

38

But just at that moment, who should happen
along but a little church mouse.
He was just as poor as poor—
as all good church mice are.
But even though his purse was empty,
his heart was filled
. . . with kindness
. . . and goodness
. . . and *plans*.

For that little church mouse, as poor as he was,
was planning a Christmas party
for all the little orphan mice who
lived in the village.

He had been busy for weeks, finding all sorts of
good things for the party. He had stored up nuts
and berries from the forest. He'd saved extra
cookies from all the kitchens around town.

He had even found a lovely green Christmas bough
in a store window. It would be just the
right size for a mouse Christmas tree.

He'd chosen some lovely pine cones and milkweed pods
to hang on it, and he had made long, bright-red
berry chains to use for festooning.

But, oh, he was worried!
The *one* thing he didn't have
was a golden *star*
for the top of his tree!

And everyone knows that the Christmas star
on top of the tree is the most important
thing of all on Christmas.

For the Christmas star
stands for all the wishes and hopes
that everyone has in his heart
for the coming year!

The Little Church Mouse was unhappy!
    Without a star, it just wouldn't seem
        like Christmas!

Then, as he scurried through the darkness,
    his shiny black eyes caught the faint glow
        of gold in that big box
            of discarded things.

"What is that?" he thought, and was about to hurry on.
    "Better look," he reasoned, thriftily.
        "It may be something I can use."
    Peeking carefully into the box,
        he saw the tarnished star!

Gently, he lifted it out and dusted it off.
    "Not bad," he murmured. "A little the worse
        for wear, perhaps. But, maybe, with
            a little glue . . . and a little paint—"

And off he scampered to his workshop with
the little star tucked safely in his arms.

All night long he worked in his workshop getting
things ready for the orphan mice children's
Christmas party.

In the morning . . . just as the golden sun was
lifting its head above the snowy hills,
all the little mice woke up
and hurried in to see the Christmas tree!

And *there*, shining brightly and proudly
atop the lovely, tall, green tree,
was the happiest Christmas star that ever was!

As the children played, and opened their gifts,
and munched their Christmas cookies,
the Little Church Mouse
looked up at the tree
and chuckled to himself.

"Yes," he said, "that's the *best* Christmas star
we've ever had, if I do say so myself.
And, you know, Christmas isn't Christmas
without a Christmas star!"

SLUMBER SONG

Good-by to all the stories now.
The sun has set, the shadows fall.
The stars, like candles,
          light the blue.
A downy pillow waits for you.
The quilt is tucked about your bed.
And so . . . to dreams,
          sweet sleepyhead!